I0537709

Seven White Wolves

CHANTÉ MCCOY

Quaking Aspen

SEVEN WHITE WOLVES

This book is a work of fiction. Names, characters, places, and incidents are the product of the author's imagination or are used fictitiously. Any resemblance to actual events, locales, or persons, living or dead, is coincidental.

Copyright © 2014 by Chanté McCoy

All Rights Reserved. No part of this book may be reproduced or transmitted in any form or by any means, electronic or mechanical, including photocopying, recording, or by any information storage and retrieval system, without written permission from the author. For information, send request via www.chantemccoy.com.

Quaking Aspen Publishing
Salt Lake City, UT

ISBN-13: 978-0989165730
ISBN-10: 0989165736

Publisher's Cataloging-in-Publication Data

McCoy, Chante, 1966-
    Seven white wolves / Chante McCoy.
    pages cm
    ISBN: 978-0-9891657-3-0 (pbk.)
    ISBN: 978-0-9891657-0-9 (e-book)
    1. Witches—Fiction. 2. Wolves—Fiction. 3. Murder—
Fiction. 4. Middle Ages—Fiction. 5. Fairy tales.
I. Title.
PS3613.C3839 S48 2014
813—dc23
                                        2014900756

January 2014
10 9 8 7 6 5 4 3 2 1

Dedication

To Karen B. McCoy,
mother and confidante,
whose faith and unfailing support
have buttressed my writing endeavors
since I was a child

Acknowledgements

Many thanks to those who have reviewed various renditions of this story, including my mother, husband, and son (who were obligated to read by virtue of our relationships) and not-so-obligated yet generous friends, including Christine McMillan, Matt Bailey, Bob Laird, and Jim Winward. I greatly valued all your insights and suggestions.

A slightly modified version of this story featured in *Spec the Halls* (2011), a charity anthology published by Alliteration Ink, with proceeds going to Heifer International. A special thanks to the editor, Steven Saus, for its inclusion.

Hints of Treacle

Like a tree calls to the bird and the ground to the rain, the window calls to me. With my shawl wrapped tightly, I walk toward it, rapt as if magicked. But no enchantment seduces me, only the scent of gingerbread and the howling of wolves.

While the villagers wince at the call of the wild dogs, their mournful song moves me to smile, an unexpected pleasure on this day. I picture them in the distance, their heads thrown back as they send their pleas skyward. I wish I could join their chorus and give voice to the pain in my heart too. Alas, I cannot utter even a small cry. I reach up to the bars and slump against the cold granite wall of my cell. Only tears speak for me, the taste of salt bitter on my chapped lips.

The hints of treacle, mixed with the tang of cloves and ginger, drift from my mother's kitchen. I imagine she and her scullions busily press the dough into wooden molds of Mama's design, creating trees and animals. In my mind's eye, I can see the little beasts, domestic and wild, and evergreens, glazed with white icing. In Mama's kitchen, she recreates the world in cookies.

Their scent heralds Mōdranicht – Mother Night – when we feast Frau Holda, our loving protectress, on the eve of the new year. Mōdranicht must be but a day or two away now. Along with the feast, the gingerbread will be served to celebrate the return of the sun after our darkest days. Then Yule and the twelve-day celebrations will begin.

We feast Frau Holda first to see us through the months ahead. In sacrifice, we slay the animals that would not survive the cold and famine, and she keeps their meat cold and our bellies fed.

For weeks, Frau Holda, draped in white, has walked the land, leaving a mantle of snow in her footsteps. In years past, I brought in fir and pine to welcome her coming, stringing garlands of greenery over the mantles and doorways and window ledges. I built an altar of flat stones, burning the boughs in Frau Holda's honor, the fragrance wafting to her realm above.

Ah, evergreen. Forests of birch. Sparkling expanses of snow. How I long to be outdoors. Whereas others retreat indoors, huddling in their huts to await for the greening of spring, the dark half of the year speaks to me. I've long loved its raw beauty, stripped of leafy ornaments. The quiet of the winter woods. The serenity of sifting flakes. I walked

2

the mountain forests alone or with my brothers. Frau Holda watched over us. She protects them even now.

These days, time passes like one long night for me, without the white of snow fields. Even with Mōdranicht approaching, I feel no childish excitement. This year, the gingerbread signals a baneful ceremony. Mōdranicht will mark my death. In the great bonfire recalling the sun, I am to burn.

I have little time left. I must hurry, get beyond my doleful mood. Besides, tears shed as easily at the spindle and loom.

Lebkuchen

Back in the far corner, I huddle from the wind free to blow through the bars. I pull on my worn kid gloves and grab a pull of limp wolfsbane, the yellow-hooded flowers long lost to a memory of summer. Now, I hold only the stems and their deep green leaves, edged with jagged teeth, darkening now that they decay. They still smell wet and sour, not yet cured and dried by time.

I roll the spindle on my thigh, then drop it, whirling and twisting the stalks. The weight of the disc whorl keeps the spindle steady and spinning. A short length of finished cord winds on the top part of the stick. I repeat, drawing out more fiber, roll, whirl, and twist. Pathetic little cord wraps on the spindle. Yet, I am almost done. Beside me, in a small pile, six shirts lie finished, their green turned brown, ragged edged from the stem ends. No soft flax in the fiber. Only the toxic bane of the animals I love most.

The harsh rattle of a key in the large iron lock rouses me from the lull of repetition and the mesmerizing spin. The heavy door pushes open, groaning on its hinges. The gaoler

4

Hans escorts in my mother, wrapped in a shawl to warm her on the walk across the castle green. She lifts the cloth over a basket and rewards him with a gingerbread horse. He thanks her with a nod and withdraws, the turning of the key locking her in with me.

She keeps her shawl tightly wrapped to shield against the chill within my cell. Melting snowflakes glisten in her hair. "Veleda," she chides. "Come away for a moment. I brought you Lebkuchen. Come. Eat. It will do you good."

I'm reluctant to do so. The last shirt lacks sleeves, and the woven fabric on the loom is too little. I wish I could ask Mama how much time I have left. One day? Two?

But I'm grateful for her company and hungry. I remove my poison-covered gloves and accept her offer with a smile. I bite into a little lamb cookie, fresh from the oven and not yet hard, the crisp ginger washing over my tongue.

My mother takes my free hand gently in hers and turns it palm side up, studying it with her eyes and own hands. One of my fingers bleeds, although my hands are callused and thick from years of spinning and weaving the unforgivable wolfsbane. In the cold, my skin cracks.

Mama scowls and raises her saddened eyes to look into mine. "Veleda, I will never understand. Why do you do this

5

to yourself? Surely, on your last days, you can give this a rest."

What else would I do, I think to myself. I pull my hand back, and my eyes wander to my spindle. I should return to my work.

Mama must have read my thoughts. Tears well in her eyes, and she blinks rapidly. "No, no, Veleda. Sit with me. Look, I brought some mulled wine for dunking. Your father will not mind I raided his cellar early." She pats the stone floor beside her.

While thoughts of my task nag at me, I nod, torn by her need. I was a mother too. I understand.

As I sit down beside her, she pulls out a glazed flagon with a leather cap, untying the thong wrapping it in place. She pours the sweet ruby wine into a mug. "Drink. Here's another cookie."

This biscuit looks like a wolf, sugared white like my brothers. I'm hesitant to eat it.

"It's not going to bite you," Mama says playfully.

I can't explain. Instead, I dunk the wolf, turning it ruddy red, a more palatable color, and nibble on the legs until it is unrecognizable and safe to eat. I eat two more Lebkuchen. Mama quietly watches me. I kiss her cheek in thanks and start to rise to return to my work.

"Veleda, wait," my mother asks. "Look at me. Is there nothing I can do? Perhaps there is still time. It is too late for your babe, but you can save yourself." She stumbles over the words in her haste. "I can't bear to lose you. There must be something.... You must speak up, talk to the king. Surely your tongue still works, and you remember the words. Even the Christian monk says you can, and I know more plant lore than that Roman."

Her voice breaks, and she furtively reaches up to brush away her tears. "If only you'd talk. Explain what happened. You're innocent. Unto my dying day, I could never believe otherwise. You're gentle and kind. No murderer. I know how much you loved that child. He was everything to you. How these fools cannot see that, I do not know."

My own tears flow afresh. I lower my head, my throat tightens, and I can barely swallow her words. At least she believes in me, knows my true heart. And that hurts me too, knowing how this bewilders and pains her.

"It must be those ravenous wolves," Mama continues.

My head swivels back, my eyes wide.

"Perhaps the queen was right about them. Their tracks are always in the village. Skulking about. Brazen. Their

7

tracks were even found in the courtyard, outside your very window."

I grab Mama's hands and, gazing into her reddened eyes, steadily shake my head. *No, Mama*, I say in my head. *It wasn't them.*

"Then who, Veleda? What?" Mama pauses, looking around even though no one else is present, then speaks in a low voice. "I'd say the queen, but why would she? You married off. Your son was no threat to her."

I shrug. Mama named her, the woman who stole my child, my suckling babe only beginning to hold his head on his own. She killed him too, all to frame me. Even my husband believed her lies, craven that he is. But the fabric has been woven. Three moons have waxed and waned. I accept his loss and my fate, so why confirm Mama's suspicion? She can do naught. If she spoke against the queen, she would join me in the fire.

Mama was right to suspect the queen all those years ago when my brothers disappeared. But Mama's talisman of protection—the pouch of valerian, yarrow, salt, and twig of rowan—only went so far, dooming me instead to a different kind of curse. The queen was too clever. She knew the black craft. I was naïve and a fool.

8

Now, Mama can do nothing more than resign herself like me.

"Veleda?" she asks, sensing my hesitation.

Resolved to go to my grave with the queen's secret as tight as my lips, I silently mouth the only answer I can give. "No."

"And you won't speak to your innocence?"

Another shake.

Her shoulders slump. "Well, if I can do nothing here, I should return to the kitchen. There's still the feast that must be made for these…these vermin who would see you…" she stops, unable to say the words. *Burn. Die.* "I hope they choke on the bones. I will never again celebrate the return of the sun. Never. For me, these will always be dark days."

I stroke her hair to calm her. I kiss her forehead to tell her I love her. She takes a deep breath and smiles weakly.

"Oh," she says. "I almost forgot." She wraps the cloth covering the basket around her hand, and, from within its depths, withdraws a handful of wolfsbane. "The last of the garden harvest. I suppose it's just as well." She also pulls out a clay jar, filled to the rim with a familiar salve of beeswax, burdock root, comfrey, chickweed, and chase-devil to counter the burns and blisters of wolfsbane.

9

With a sigh, she knocks at the door. "Fare well, Veleda. I'll return before tomorrow night. I have white mandrake root for you to stupefy and deaden the pain of the flames. I know not what else to do."

The look on her face causes me to turn away. I know what she feels, having lost my own child. How strange that I will die on Mother Night. Perhaps it is fitting, turning my sentence into sacrifice, as done in the days of old.

White Wolves

Tomorrow night then. Less than a day to complete my task. No sleep will close my eyes tonight, even if I must spin and weave in the dark. I knock on the cell door. Hans peers in, a face I've known since childhood. In the dirt on the floor, I draw a candle with a teardrop flame and look at him questioningly.

While I am his prisoner, I once thought Hans a friend, quick with a greeting and a kind word, and I'd bring him treats from my mother's kitchen. And, now, while my life is forfeit, the king allowed my spindle and loom to accompany me in my cell, and provided woolen blankets and furs for my warmth with an admonition to treat me gently. I hope he will agree to my plea.

"Do you wish a candle, Lady Veleda?"

I eagerly nod and hold up my hands, the fingers splayed wide.

"Ten candles?"

I smile even wider. Tallow and flame will see me through the night. Perhaps my brothers will visit again.

11

SEVEN WHITE WOLVES

How strange I never knew that the seven boys, who played Blindman's Bluff with me in the gardens and castle halls, were my half-brothers until after they had long disappeared. Those young boys were simply my friends, pranksters tugging my braids and comforters patting my shoulder when I skinned a knee. Looking at each other, we never guessed our kinship. My red hair flamed next to their blond, for I favored my mother and they theirs, the first queen of the king.

I was the age of the middle boy, with the eldest only a few years taller. The queen died in childbirth with Jerg. I remember him as a five-year-old, a towheaded shadow who gobbled cookies and cakes as soon as they emerged from Mama's ovens. The oldest, Mathÿs, I eyed shyly, a handsome youth growing into a Nordic god but who hardly noticed a thin stick of a girl whose blood had yet to flow.

The guards side-stepped our flurry, and the servants uprighted furniture and readjusted tapestries in our wake...until the day they were no longer there.

Another wife stood by the king that fateful day, and she shed no tears. A dark-skinned beauty from a southern kingdom, the new queen was exotic, ambitious, and vain. In the springtime of her life, she planned to birth babes of her

12

own and place them in the heart of the king.

The white wolves appeared on the fray of the castle grounds that day, beautiful snow-colored beasts, unlike their smoky, black-tipped cousins. But no one connected the boys' disappearance with the wolves. Instead, the guards aimed their arrows at them, and the wolves fled into the forest.

The entire castle searched the grounds high and low, and, for months, hunters scoured the mountain sides for the missing boys. No one could explain how they vanished. The king mourned for a year, his own golden hair turning gray with grief. The new queen bore no babe to distract him.

Unexpectedly, the king cast an eye toward me and began asking me questions. Silly things about what I liked. Kittens and candied ginger and favorite games. Distractions of little girls.

One day, he called forth his court and demanded the presence of my mother and me. Before the designated hour, a servant knocked at our little room attached to the kitchen, and bid me to remove my plain woolen gown, apron, and linen scarf. She proceeded to dress me in a tight-bodiced confection of the cloth of Damascus, in a blue that rivaled the sky. The servant plaited my hair, weaving in a strand of

13

pearls, like mistletoe berries growing from spun amber. I had no mirror but knew I transformed. Mama quaked, but I was too simple to wonder at my good fortune.

In the royal chamber, the king called me to his throne perched above his court. I glanced nervously at the hushed collection of barons, dukes, and other nobles and their ladies. The new queen stared at me, eyes wide with anger. I didn't know why. Not then. But, the king smiled widely, and I approached.

That's when I learned the king was my father.

He stood before me and cupped his hands around my face. "From this day forth, I acknowledge Veleda, daughter of Bechte, as my lawful daughter and princess of the realm."

That night, Mama gave me the amulet. She knocked on the door of my new bedroom, and gave me the little cloth pouch with a leather thong to wear about my neck.

"Always wear this, Veleda. It will protect you."

"From what, Mama?"

"No one but the king and I knew whose blood runs through you. You were safe when that knowledge was secret. Now the queen knows."

"The queen?" I asked, surprised. The woman had never spoken with me, but I admired her dusky beauty and poise,

14

thinking it a fine thing that she would be my mother too.

"Open your eyes, Veleda. Today you are no longer a child. Have you not seen the queen visit the kitchen garden? She knows the plants by name. She takes cuttings, but I know naught of her cooking nor of her healing. *I* would know. And she bottles spiders and beetles."

Mama had taught me the secrets of the plants: those that calmed stomachs and nerves, helped babies quicken, and increased a lover's desire. But of beetles, I could imagine no medicinal purpose.

"Black craft," Mama said. "The amulet will protect you against it."

"Why would she want to hurt me?"

"She loved your brothers not, nor will she you. Whatever happened to princes can happen to princesses too."

Vow

Mama's fears were well founded. My joy at discovering I was of royal blood was short-lived. The queen entered my chamber a few moons later, on the eve of Mōdranicht no less, when the king planned to introduce me to neighboring royalty and discuss possible matches at the feast.

As she approached, staring with narrowed eyes, I thought she would stab me. What she did was hardly better.

She backed me into a corner, and I waited for her knife. Instead, she threw a fine powder on me, while chanting.

> *Bark by day, howl by night*
> *Canus familiaris*
> *Now take flight.*
>
> *Into the wood hie thy hide*
> *Canus lupus lupus*
> *Wolf bona fide.*
>
> *True to form, free to roam*
> *Animalia de Canidae*
> *Never come home.*

I stood, blinking at her, the blur of words slowly sinking in. But the queen seemed more surprised to see that I

16

stayed upright, on two legs instead of four, my furless skin still my own.

"What?" she screamed with rage. "How?"

I stayed quiet, grateful for Mama's foresight, yet knowing I was still not safe.

The queen raked her hands through her hair, disheveling her carefully arranged coif. At that moment, I was struck by how shallow her beauty truly was. Her looks, so greatly admired, were but a glamour, a shell to hide what she was inside. Her face, twisted in fury, exuded hate. I saw only a hag, more frightening than the trolls in the stories the old grannies tell.

Then she damned me, telling me the truth, which I half-guessed with her shape-shifting curse.

"You should be a wolf," she hissed. "Like those horrid white beasts."

The fog of innocence lifted. I suddenly understood. The wolves on the outskirts of the castle and village...their odd snow-white coats...numbering seven...and the queen's fervor in having them hunted, a gold piece each upon their heads.

"The wolves? They are my brothers?"

"Yes, your brothers, Veleda."

17

I covered my mouth in horror.

She paused, looking at me with new intensity. "Tell me, did you know they were your brothers before I changed them into dogs?"

I shook my head, still stunned by her revelations.

"Then what do you care about what form those boys took? They could as easily be serpents slithering on the floor or birds taking to the air."

I recalled their faces, their laughter, the little quibbles among themselves. "But I loved them, even like brothers. They were my friends."

A smile tugged at the corners of her mouth. "Love.... How much do you love them, I wonder. Enough to free them?"

"Turn them back into my brothers?" I clarified.

"Yes, to their original forms. You could do it. Love is a potent magic, you know."

I should have guessed the queen planned an escape. Whatever scheme she had in mind would bring me no good. But, my brothers' lives were at stake. What else could I have done? And, if I said "no," perhaps a dagger would have fallen, after all.

So, I willingly took her bait, although, like a fish never

spotting the hook, I failed to see the bigger danger. I just saw a chance to have my seven brothers again, from Mathÿs down to little Jerg. "Tell me how," I said.

"How deliciously sweet you are, Veleda. I will tell you how. But you must decide here and now. Tomorrow, the offer no longer holds. Do you understand? If you say no, they will die as wolves do, hunted down on the mountainside."

I nodded.

"One year for each brother, you swear a vow of silence. No word, no laugh, no cry may pass your pretty little lips. In those seven mute years, you must spin and weave seven shirts, one for each brother, from the wolf's baneful herb, sacred to Hecate."

"Who?" I interrupted.

"The moon's own goddess."

"Like Máni," I said, thinking of the northern moon goddess. Wolves pursue her through the heavens, which might explain the fondness for wolfsbane. But, Frau Holda, on the eve of her Mōdranicht, also came to mind. She is a winter goddess also dressed in white, and the wolf is one of her sacred beasts, often pulling her wagon across the sky. Frau Holda frowns on wolfsbane and the poisoning of

19

wolves, but perhaps that's how it would work in the magic, killing the wolf so the man might live.

The queen looked annoyed. "Seven years of silence, seven shirts of wolfsbane, no flax nor wool woven through the warp. Do you accept?"

A terrible choice and no time to consider. Despite the chill going down my spine, I said "yes."

The queen smiled widely; she had caught her fish. "And that, my dear, is the last word you shall utter for the next seven years. No rush on the shirts, however. Wolfsbane emerges after the snowmelt, and you can only harvest once it blooms."

Yet another condition she slipped in. Sworn to silence, I could only stare, mouth gaping.

The queen looked out the window at the activity in the courtyard. Below, villagers piled faggots on a large pyre. Nearby, over red glowing coals, a pig and two bulls turned on spits, culled animals providing fresh meat for the feast. The smell of their crackling flesh wafted to the windows. Servants rushed back and forth, covering trestle tables with evergreens and candles and a parade of dishes from the kitchen where Mama marshaled a small army of bakers, butchers, and scullions. In years past, I sneaked pinches

20

from the savory dishes. The pickled herring from the great sea to the north. Loaves upon loaves of still spongy bread. Potages of chickpeas, pork, purslane, carrots, parsley, and sage. Sauerkraut with caraway. Frumenty of boiled wheat with almonds, currants, and eggs. Honey-coated candied ginger. Barrels of ale and pitchers of mulled wine and almond milk.

"Well, I must ready for the festivities," she said. "I believe this will be a good year, after all."

Hrodulf

She left. I stayed in my chamber, shocked, until a servant took me by the hand to the feast. I hardly remember the night, only that I frustrated father and his royal guests, potential wooers of my hand, with my new silence.

I adapted sooner than those around me, enduring various "cures" and nigh-endless pleading for me to talk. When I began harvesting wolfsbane, spending days wandering the mountains, then spinning the toxic weed only to weave the rough result, the court concluded I was not only mute but touched. Mama—forever loving, though equally confused—helped collect the plant, and seeded even more in her gardens.

Only my lupine brothers somehow understood. One summer day, while I walked the woods alone searching for wolfsbane, they approached. They timidly appeared behind trees, ready to flee at any abrupt move. I sat on the ground, head bowed and hands held out in invitation. They joyously bound at me, our reunion one of licks and head scratches. They were beautiful, with thick snow-white coats and blue

22

eyes, and tame with me as any hand-raised pup.

When I showed alone in the forest, they accompanied me on my walks. All of us unable to talk, we were perfect companions. I communicated with nods and shakes, smiles and frowns, and they with barks and whines, upright ears or down, tails wagging or tucked.

The queen, hedging her bets, upped the price on their pelts and rode along on royal hunts. But Frau Holda protected my brothers. No arrows hit their mark, and they were too shrewd for traps.

Despite being mute, suitors continued to woo me. Widowed kings and young princes called, willing to forgive my silence in light of my own pale beauty and budding curves. I shook my head to decline their offers, wanting to stay near my brothers and complete what I had begun. The king did not chide me. I think he was reluctant to lose his only child, for the queen had yet to bear any other heirs.

The queen wizened to my reasoning. She waggled the king's ear, insistent I should marry. Mama encouraged me to reconsider, as well, thinking I'd be safer out of the queen's reach. Mama even tried to help the queen conceive. She plied her with sunflower seeds and teas of red raspberry leaf, red cloves, and stinging nettle. In the royal bed chamber, she hung mistletoe over their bed, and created sachets of white oak bark, fennel, and dill for under their pillows.

I finally agreed to marry. One of my father's dukes caught my eye. A handsome man who smiled shyly and walked the gardens with me, holding my basket. I gladly nodded "yes" when he approached the king for my hand.

Yet, my step-mother scowled. The duke lived too close. She wanted me far away.

Within a few months of my marriage, my belly began to swell. Unlike the queen, I proved fertile. This too cinched my fate. But, for the first time in years, I was so happy, smiling at everyone, thrilled by the life within. My husband, so loving then, was like a child looking forward to a long-promised treat. He rubbed my stomach repeatedly, laughing when a hand or foot pushed back.

Even the king celebrated the birth of our baby boy, feasting us and the court for three days. How proudly I displayed that little bundle. My sweet, sweet baby boy. My husband named him Hrodulf. He had a cap of blond hair like his feral uncles, a sight that made me smile even more.

Yet again, my happiness was short lived. One morning, I awoke and found his crib empty. My brothers' paw prints were around the house, and the villagers talked of the wolves, but talk soon turned to me: the crazy mute. Then they called me a witch. They said I talked to wolves and must have fed them the flesh of my own.

My husband was distraught as me. "Speak, Veleda, you must! Tell me what happened. Dispel these untruths."

I pleaded with my eyes, but his turned suspicious. His distress turned into anger, and he slapped me and pulled my hair. "Why are you always spinning and weaving this weed? Wolfsbane, no less. The stuff of witches." Finally, he knocked me unconscious. When I awoke, he could look at me no more.

The mob petitioned the king for justice, fearing the disappearance of their own children, already afraid for them with winter soon upon us and the lengthening nights and cold. The king finally relented to keep the peace. No doubt he was unsure what to think of me too.

I returned to the castle I'd once called home, only to be sentenced to the dungeon in its depths. Despite the cold, barren cell, I was relieved to be away from my husband, but equally shamed that my father joined in my betrayal. I found I could forgive the villagers easier than those who had declared their love of me.

Final Gift

So, here I find myself, spinning the last of my wolfsbane in the early morning hours, still dark with only the flicker of my last candle to light my work. My brothers visited in the night. I couldn't see them but for a muzzle here and there when one pushed through the bars. They whimpered at my window until they fled the approach of a night guard.

I have the rest of the day to weave the fabric and stitch on the sleeves. I can only hope my brothers will find the shirts when the time comes. Mama will keep them for me.

True to her word, she comes in the evening with more Lubkuchen, mulled wine, and the promised powder of white mandrake root. I take off my gloves to enjoy my mother's company and gingerbread one last time.

Mama sits quietly this time, more composed, more resigned. We eat a couple of the white sugared trees from her kitchen. I lean into her, inhaling her scent, sweat mixed with baking aromas. She strokes her hand over my hair. When she speaks, it's but a whisper.

"Oh, Veleda, this should never happen. It is not proper for a child to die before a parent. You know this." Her voice cracks. After a pause, she forges on, a woman carrying a heavy burden but determined to reach the end of a journey.

"I will go to my grave, believing in your innocence. I can only hope I will see you in the next world. Fear not," she tells me, trying to convince herself as well as me. "If the Roman has the right of it, perhaps it will be the Christian heaven. The monks says it's like Valhalla but even women may go, not just warriors. Even if it's nothing more, how bad can that be? Maybe life and death are like a swallow swooping out of a freezing night into a warm banquet hall full of merriment, and then out again into the night."

I tightly hug Mama. I hope she forgives me. At the moment, I'm not sure what I've done, having lost my only child and with no assurance of saving my brothers from their fate. Was all in vain? My brothers may linger, trapped in bodies of beasts for life when I die.

My mother and I ease apart. A sound outside the door draws her eye.

"I must go now. Hans says I cannot stay long. Veleda, look here, listen well. Save the wine until you see the moon from the window. Pour in half the powder, the pain will be

27

less. Pour all the powder in, and visions will take your mind. Only your body will leave this cell. I threw water on the bonfire wood, so the smoke will kill you before the flames. Do you understand?"

I nod. She gives me her last gift: an easier way to exit the world, and I am again touched by her love for me. But I am reluctant to accept the gift, wanting to hold on to the end. I hope to see my brothers yet one more time.

Mama leaves, tears finally escaping as Hans leads her away. I take up the last unfinished shirt. One sleeve is on, but I'm short of fabric for the second. I sew on what little is left. I have no more wolfsbane to spin, no cord to weave, no extra rough cloth to complete below the elbow. I sigh, sorrow heavy in my heart. In the end, I failed to complete my task.

"Lady Veleda," Hans says through the door. "We leave within the hour."

I look about, unsure of what to do with my few minutes left. I eye the wine and powder. *Half*, I decide. I lack the courage to face the flames without my mother's help. I finish the wine too, and pray to Frau Holda I allowed enough time for the mandrake root to take effect.

When the key turns in the door, I gather up the

wolfsbane shirts, all that I have to show for my years of silence. The shirts smell of summer faded to fall with hints of hay and the thick loam of the forest floor. My first woven shirt crumbled years ago from drying—no doubt a deliberate slip of the witch to not mention the brittle results—and now the shirts also smell of lard, with animal fat rubbed into the fabric to keep it pliant and whole. I only hope the grease doesn't interfere with the spell, but I had no other way to preserve the shirts for so long.

Even without my added touches, I've often wondered if the shirts will truly work. What if it was all a ruse? A distraction to give false hope? But hope I must, for I have nothing else left.

Hans stands at the doorway, now my executioner to escort me to my death. He holds up some rope, his face bunched questioningly. I realize he's asking to bind my hands. I shake my head slightly and blink my eyes. *No, I will not fight you*, I try to say. *Let me walk freely.* He understands and directs me to walk ahead, and I step forward with my wolfsbane shirts in my hands.

The dungeon halls are dimly lit. As I step out into the night, I am blinded by the torches of the waiting villagers, all crowding around, hoping for a glimpse of the witch who murdered her own babe. If only they knew who the real witch was.

Bonfire

They boo and hiss as I walk forward. "Witch," I hear. "Child killer! Burn her!" Fear and anger consume them. They—the very people I've known since a child—would readily throw me to the wolves: themselves. Although they have no fur, their fear makes them more deadly than any fanged beast.

"Move back, move wide," Hans tells those pressing in.

A rotting carrot hits the side of my head. A foul-smelling spray runs down my neck. For a moment, I am stunned. How they must hate me to waste precious food, even if fodder only fit for pigs. A few others throw stones, but just as many hit Hans and the other guards who gesture threateningly back at the crowd. One slices my cheek. I feel its sting and the wet trickle of blood.

I wonder what Frau Holda thinks, if the gods still want human sacrifices. Are not cattle and swine enough? Ahead, the circle of wood awaits me, the kindling and logs piled high. In its center, a single tall trunk points to the sky: the stake. A shudder wracks by body as I look upon my funeral

31

pyre. Hans still carries the rope with which to tie me to it. I will invite that binding, least I flee in terror.

The wine and powder are taking affect. I feel like I'm walking in a dream. With each step, I care less that death meets me at the end. The world's taking on a glaze, like those white iced cookies. Even seeing the king, queen, and Mama at the end of the gauntlet jars me little. Something is important about Mama, though. I must remember. *Oh, yes, the shirts*. I must give them to her for safe keeping.

The crowd still screams, but I no longer hear their words. Only their noise, like rolling thunder all around me. I keep my eyes on Mama. She cries but waits for me. *She's brave*, I think, doubtful I could have watched Hrodulf burn.

As I near, I hold out the shirts to her. Suddenly, the queen looms in front of me. "I think not, red-headed witch. Your black charms burn with you."

"Witch, witch," the crowd choruses, picking up on her words.

I look to the king to plead, but his head is bowed, eyes averted. My last request denied. In a flickering moment of lucidity, I realize all my work, my brothers' hopes, will go up in flames. I stubbornly balk, but, at a gesture from the queen, two guards place themselves between me and Mama.

32

Hans nudges me forward. Closer and closer to the stake. Shirts still in my arms, he ties me to the rough hewn fir log. Its pores exude sap, reminding me of happy evergreen memories through my fogging brain.

"Sorry, Lady Veleda," he whispers, then turns away. A guard waits to the side, holding a burning torch. He passes it to Hans.

The people step back. The circle widens. Finally, silence. The torch touches the kindling. The dark night lights up. Flames race around me. Roaring. Oranges and yellows lick the sky. The winter night feels as warm as a midsummer day. I close my eyes.

Then, I hear screams. Not mine. Outside. I open my eyes, faintly curious. The villagers are running. White wolves. White teeth. Coming toward me. They snarl and snap. All make way.

Frau Holda! Of course. They bring her. Her sacred night. The goddess of spinning. The Mother Goddess too. I forget. Her wagon must be close behind.

Wolves paw at the wood. Burning sticks sizzle in the snow. Two leap the fiery hurdle. One chews on the ropes. *Brother?* I wonder. Is he one of Frau Holda's own? Even with my mind muddled, I remember the shirts. I throw one at it. A smoky moment later, a tall blonde young man appears. Naked as the day he was born. The wolf gone.

He works the knots holding me. "Throw the others," he reminds me.

Oh, yes, I think. I throw another. The shirt transforms the other near wolf. Another young man rises in the haze.

"The shirts, Veleda! We need them all."

Yes, yes. I dole them. I hit each wolf with a marksman's accuracy. The last wolf stands over the queen. She lies in the snow. Blood from her throat flows. White becomes crimson. A blossoming winter rose.

And I see *her*. Beautiful. Moonlit hair dragging the snow. Dressed in shimmering white. Sparkling like a field of snow on a bright day. Frau Holda. I knew it. The wolves brought her. She came.

She smiles at me. My eyes burn. I squint to see her. I smile back.

Frau Holda fades in the fog of smoke. An acrid smell in my nose. In my throat. Choking.

The man coughs. Blue eyes blinking. *Mathÿs?* I wonder. *Why is he here?*

He curses, upset, fumbling. I look down. How odd. One hand a man's. The other a paw. Fur white. White. White.

My head floats. Higher. Lighter. To the stars. My body. A weight.

"Veleda! Don't go."

A tear on my face. I try to look. To see.

Light becomes a pinhole. All black. Dark sleep.

Next World

When my eyes open, the bonfire seems but a remnant of a fever dream. Sitting up in my old feather bed, I think it might be. I remember Frau Holda. And the wolves. My brothers…

I lean back, shaking my head.

"Veleda?" My mother sits beside the bed. "Thank the gods. Guard!" The door opens. "Tell the king she awakes."

I stare at her, still unsure of what is real and what is not. Perhaps a mandrake root vision. Or is this the next world?

Mama grabs my hand and looks intently at me. "My girl, my girl. I worried you were lost to us after all. Are you in pain?

I shake my head.

"Good, good. All will be well now. The queen is dead, and you are safe. I swear."

Then it wasn't a dream. I look around me more carefully now, but I only see Mama in my room.

"And your brothers have come back, Veleda. They told us all."

That was what I wished to hear. I relax and settle back into my bed. *Mōdranicht fulfilled its promise*, I think. The sun has returned.

My brothers, older than remembered, enter the room. The eldest are now young men, the youngest grown into youths tall and strong. I know each of their names. I also recognize their eyes, still wild and wary. Awkwardly they stand about, until the youngest leaps forth to hug me. The others follow, until the oldest reaches for his turn.

I stare horrified, remembering the unfinished shirt. It's Mathÿs, who received the first shirt on my pile. A paw extends from his shirt sleeve, with talons long as my littlest finger and fur the color of frost.

"I shall bear it proudly, sister. Do not worry. Besides, there are times when a strong paw is better than a hand."

The king arrives at the open door, surprising all but my mother. And how he has changed. The grey in his hair has doubled, aging him by years. Even more than this, his manner is...meeker, subdued. He motions my brothers aside and approaches my bed. I expect my brothers to step aside. Instead, they gather round and growl a low warning.

Mama stands, so he may take her chair. "Veleda, daughter, how I have wronged you and nearly lost all by my

37

foolishness." His voice has lost its old confidence. "How shamed I am by that woman I called 'wife'. She bespelled me, tangled me in her lies. Can you ever forgive me and my doubting heart?"

I feel a pang of anger at this man who calls himself my father. Unlike my mother who stood by me, I almost died by his command. Hard to understand, even if he was misled by false beauty. At least *she* is gone, her deceit discovered, and my brothers stand before me as young men. My innocence is clear. *But, he* is *the king*. I smile obediently. He seems pleased.

I hear the wails of a babe beyond my walls and remember my greater loss. Sadness weighs on the moment of happiness. The spark extinguishes in the winter chill.

The door opens again. In walks my husband, the man who no longer wanted to see me. The man who beat me. As with my father, my thoughts are not kind. I don't know what to think of the duke with whom I shared a bed. I only know I will never do so again.

He holds a cloth bundle and offers it to me. At first, I turn my head from him, but a small movement catches my eye. Then my heart about breaks from my breast, now whole and beating hard. I can hardly believe what I hold in my arms. Little Hrodulf, stirring fretfully in his swaddling. So much bigger than I remember him. Alive. Safe. I embrace him tightly, afraid he is but a figment of a dream.

Young Jerg peers down on the swaddled babe. "We followed the queen the night she took the baby. We stole him back."

"Yes," another brother says. "A she-wolf suckled him. Nursed him with her litter as one of her own."

Mama leans over. "Veleda, what do you think? Can you speak now?"

I utter my first words in seven long years. "He's beautiful," I say, whispering. "Worth it all."

About the Author

At any given time, Chanté McCoy is reading a handful of novels, taking a continuing education class to dabble in her latest interest or hiking the mountains of Utah with Elvis, her 110-lb Doberman Pinscher. While generally indulging in her love of fantasy, she writes in other genres too. Visit chantemccoy.com to follow her blog.

*****

Did you enjoy the book? Please tell a friend and leave a review on Amazon, Goodreads, Facebook, or wherever you think is appropriate. Reviews mean the world to an author.

www.ingramcontent.com/pod-product-compliance
Lightning Source LLC
Chambersburg PA
CBHW071221130626
46555CB00004B/1788